METER
THIS WAY
THAT WAY
YES
NO
NOT AFRAID
TEACHERS
CLOWNS
ALIENS
CLOSETS AT NIGHT
SIDEWALK CRACKS
TEMPERATURE GAUGE
EE LEVER
EXTREME EMERGENCY
JUST BARELY
NO BITING
AS A MOUSE
AS A BOMB
QUIET
OWN
5000°
5 SECOND WARNING
CHINA SYNDROME

Jamie Lee Curtis & Laura Cornell

It's Hard to Be Five

Learning How to Work My Control Panel

Joanna Cotler Books
An Imprint of HarperCollinsPublishers

I would like to give a HIGH FIVE to Joanna and Laura, my creative comrades, Phyllis, Kelly, Justin, Melissa, Alicia, Lucille and everyone at HarperCollins and a Special Everest HIGH FIVE to Thomas—just for being you.
—J.L.C.

I am grateful for the quintet that surrounds and makes me— Jamie, Joanna, Justin, Melissa and Alicia— and beyond—all at the great HarperCollins.
—L.C.

It's Hard to Be Five: Learning How to Work My Control Panel
 www.harperchildrens.com
Library of Congress Cataloging-in-Publication Data Curtis, Jamie Lee. It's hard to be five : learning how to work my control panel / by Jamie Lee Curtis & Laura Cornell.— 1st ed. p. cm.
Summary: A child finds that learning to have self-control is hard, but it can also be fun.
ISBN 0-06-008095-7 — ISBN 0-06-008096-5 (lib. bdg.) [1. Growth—Fiction. 2. Stories in rhyme.]
I. Title: It is hard to be five. II. Cornell, Laura, ill. III. Title. PZ8.3.C93471t 2004 2003024187 [E]—dc22
Designed by Alicia Mikles 3 4 5 6 7 8 9 10

For Robert Brandt, my dad
—J.L.C.

For Barbara and Neal who gave me
the best and easiest "5 years old"
—L.C.

CLOWNS
5 and up
Friends with Scary Things SERIES
INCLUDES: WIG, GLOVES, SHOES, NOSE, FACE PAINT, DOTS, JOKE BOOK, BALLOONS
ALIENS
DETECTOR
5
Look, no ears! And though he may have a scary look, he's friendly as can be.
He may have only one eye, but he's cute as a button, and a little like a green tomato.
FIVE IS Hard Soft (ha ha)
"THE MOST IMPORTANT POCKETBOOK YOU'LL EVER BUY."
YOU ARE THERE
WHAT THIS MEANS

It's **hard** to be five.
I'm little no more.
Good old days are gone.
'Bye

one,

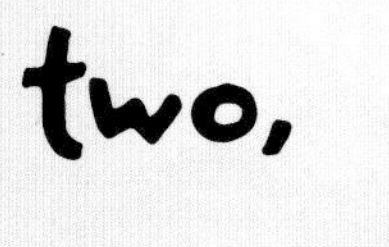

two,

three,

four.

It's hard to be five. Just yelled at my brother.
My mind says do one thing,
my mouth says another.
Would you ever so kindly please give me my wig back?
IT'S MINE!
Perhaps an offer of just a small taste would be nice.
GIVE IT!
Let's see. It's been an hour and nine minutes. Might I have a smidge of a turn before we have to leave?
MOM!

It's hard to be five. I've got to keep going.
My clothes can't keep up 'cause my body keeps growing.

At five I hear **NO** and **DON'T**—I can't win!—
when balls bowl inside at my ten juice-box pins.

I'd rather hear TRY IT and SURE, I confess . . .

. . . and if dirt is involved, a very loud

YES!

It's hard to be five.
Parents want you all clean.

But washing my face makes me

crabby and mean.

It's hard to be five.
All I want is to play.
I'm starting at school,
and I don't get a say.
School seems so scary.
School seems so strange.
I'm only five.
My whole world's going to change.

5
and
Lovin'
5th
BATTALION
FREE
2B

It's hard to be five and wanting to hit
when Scott **cuts** in line and says **I** did it.

At five I do things that I don't mean to do,
like when I **bit** Jake 'cause **he** cut in line too.

It's hard to be five.
It takes Superman skill.
Sitting in circles.
Sitting so still.

Sitting still.

Still sitting still.

Still

Sitting

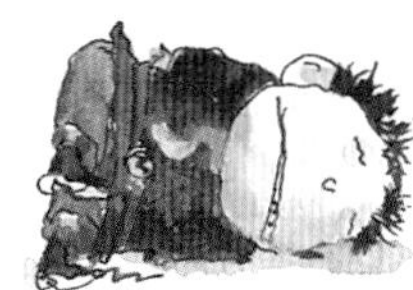

still.

SIT
STILL!

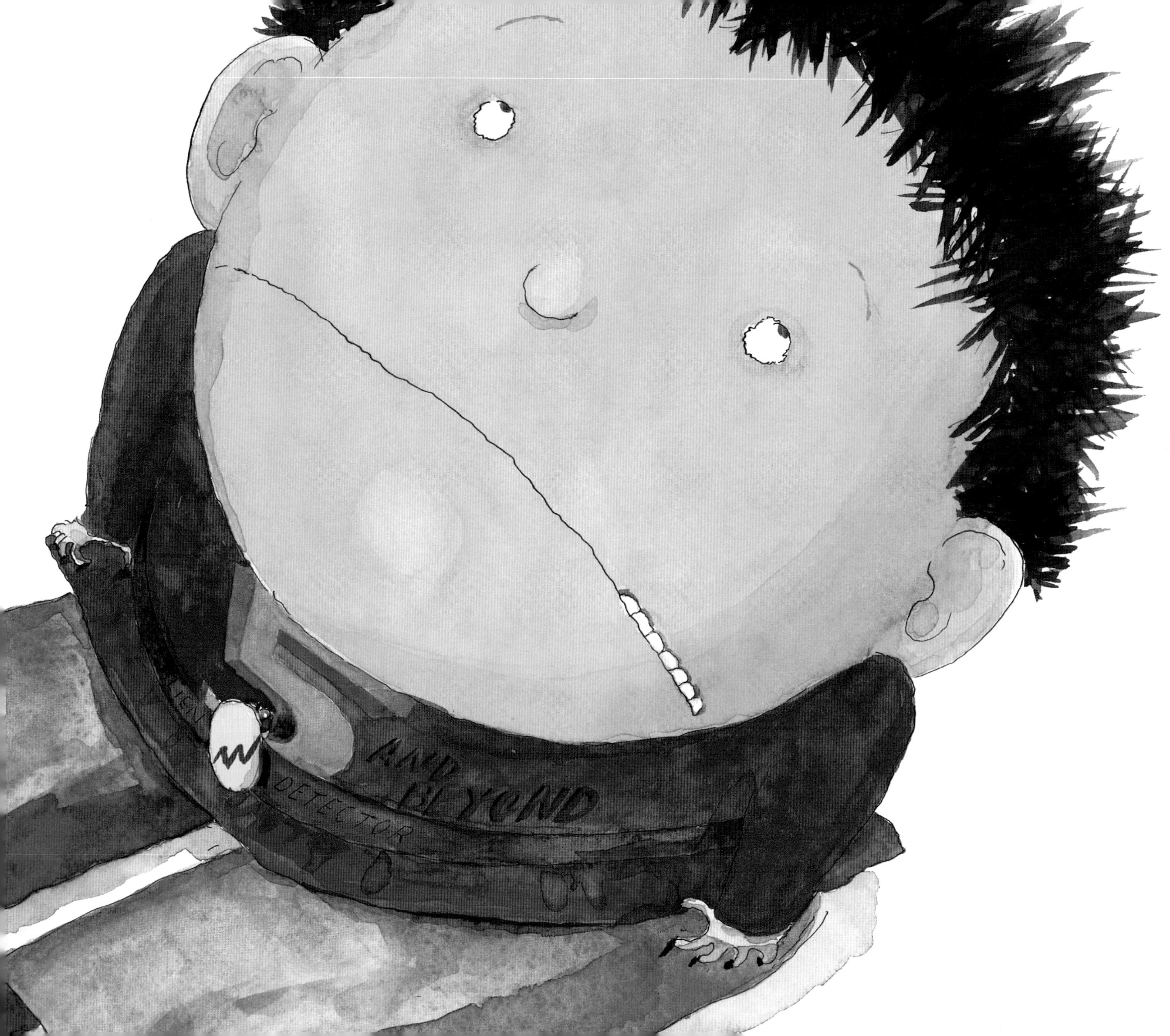
AND BEYOND
DETECTOR

And then there's the **walking** all by myself,
only picked up to reach a high shelf.

I walk to the park.

I walk to the school.

I walk to the bus.

I walk to the pool.

I walk to karate.
I walk with closed eyes.
I walk like
a ninja
chopping
bad guys.
5
5

It's **fun** to be five!

Big changes are here!

My body's my car,
and I'm **licensed** to steer.

At five I'm a worker—a bee among bees.

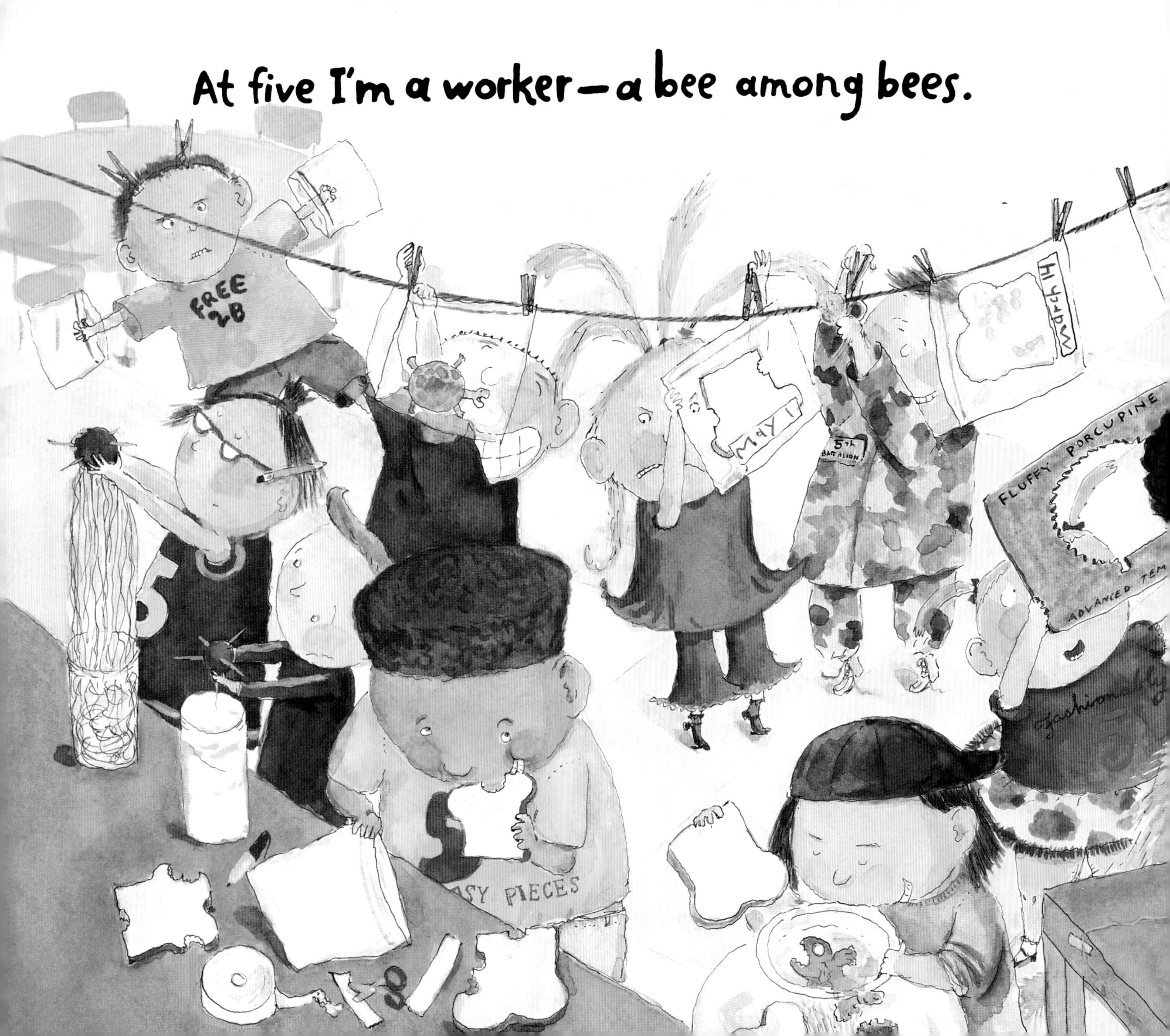

I build things and grow things, say thank you and please.

Some **fun** things are hard.

And some **hard** things are fun.

I know when to **walk**.

I know when to **run**.

I know when to **stop.**

And I know when to **go.**

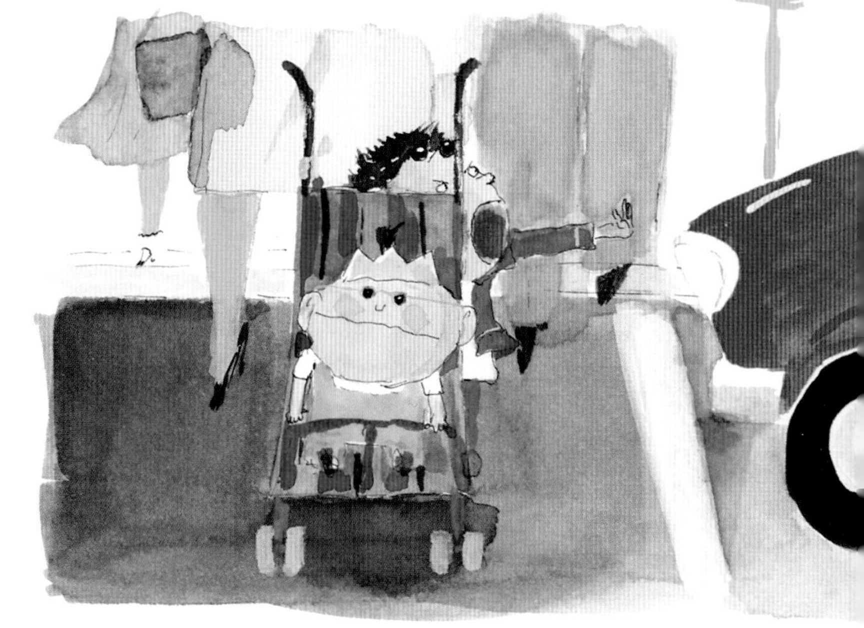

I know when to **push.**

And I know when to **tow.**

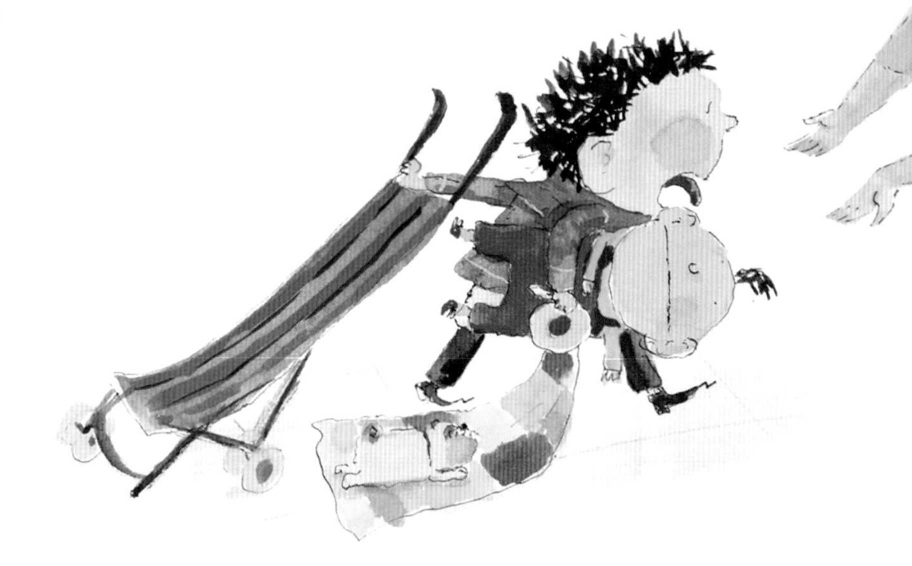

DARE 2B 5
DRIVER LICENSE
CLASS:
HEIGHT: 3'8½" WEIGHT: 46 LBS
HAIR: COOL
EYES: X-RAY
FAVORITE COLOR: RED
FAVORITE FOOD: REFRIED BEANS
FAVORITE MOVIE: THE SOUND OF MUSIC
FRAMABLE MAP
Five(5)
In Iceland a 5-year-old mines for ice.
In England a 5-year-old is becoming a king or queen.
In the United States a 5-year-old is learning to tie his shoes.
In South America a 5-year-old is helping to save the rain forest.

At five I can lie down alone in my bed
and dream of my past and my future ahead.
And when I mess up or do right, it's a start,
'cause I have my own mind
and I have my own heart.

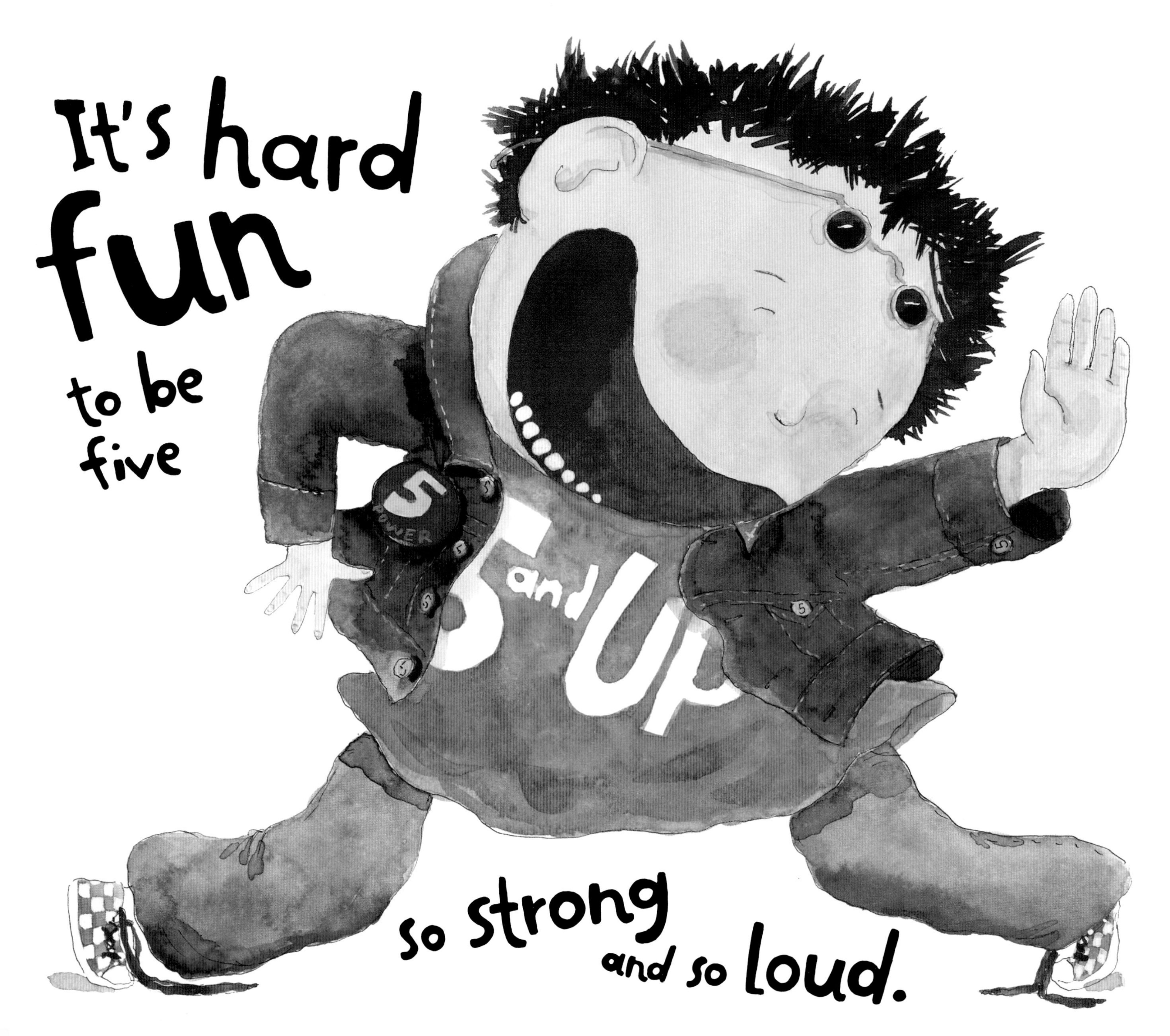
It's hard
fun
to be
five
5
POWER
5
and
Up
so strong
and so loud.

Give me five
'cause I know it.

I'm here and I'm
PROUD!

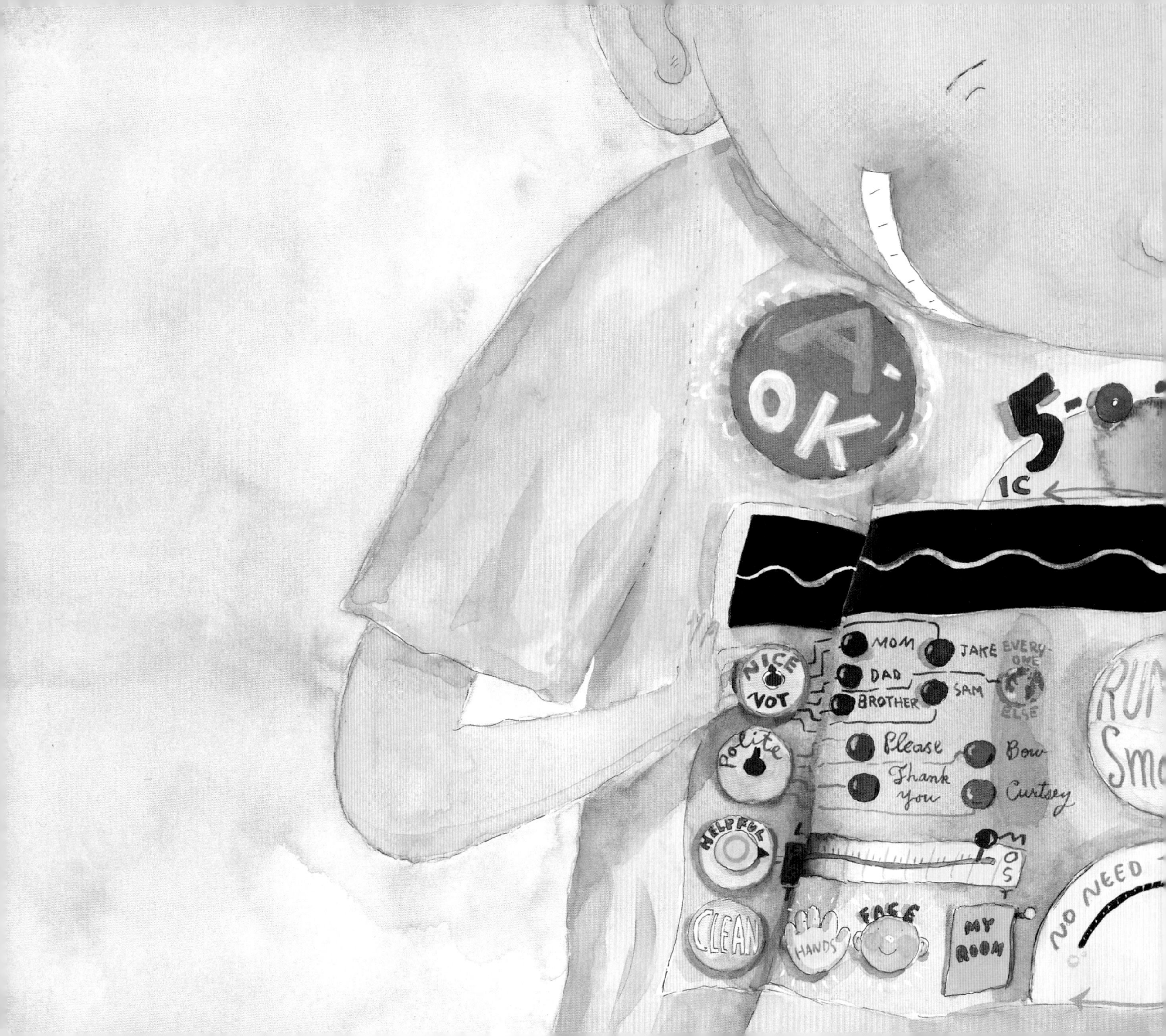
A-OK
NICE
NOT
MOM
JAKE
DAD
SAM
BROTHER
EVERY-ONE ELSE
Polite
Please
Bow
Thank you
Curtsey
HELPFUL
CLEAN
HANDS
FACE
MY ROOM
NO NEED